# The
# Crazy Key

"Let's go downstairs," Bess said. "I smell pancakes."

Nancy turned toward the stairs. Then she stopped in her tracks. "Hey," she said, pointing, "look at that."

"What?" Bess asked, following Nancy's gaze.

"That old trunk," Nancy said. "See the shape of the lock? It's a heart, just like the heart shape on the key Chip found."

Bess gasped with excitement. She and George ran over to the trunk.

"You're right!" George said. "And the keyhole is the same size as that crazy old key!"

**The Nancy Drew Notebooks**

Available from MINSTREL Books

#15

# THE NANCY DREW NOTEBOOKS®

# THE CRAZY KEY CLUE

## CAROLYN KEENE

Illustrated by Anthony Accardo

A MINSTREL® BOOK

PUBLISHED BY POCKET BOOKS

New York   London   Toronto   Sydney   Tokyo   Singapore

A MINSTREL PAPERBACK *Original*

 A Minstrel Book published by
POCKET BOOKS, a division of Simon & Schuster Inc.
1230 Avenue of the Americas, New York, NY 10020

Copyright © 1996 by Simon & Schuster Inc.
Produced by Mega-Books of New York, Inc.

ISBN: 0-671-56859-0

First Minstrel Books printing November 1996

10  9  8  7  6  5  4  3  2  1

NANCY DREW, THE NANCY DREW NOTEBOOKS,
A MINSTREL BOOK and colophon are registered trademarks of
Simon & Schuster Inc.

Cover art by Aleta Jenks

Printed in the U.S.A.

# THE CRAZY KEY CLUE

# 1
# Finders Keepers

**H**ey, stop! You're getting leaves in my hair!" Bess Marvin shouted.

Nancy Drew laughed at her best friend. Then she picked up another handful of dried leaves. She tossed them up in the air. They fluttered onto her own head as they fell to the ground.

"I just raked those," Bess said. She put her hands on her hips.

"No, you didn't," George Fayne said to her cousin. "*I* raked them."

Nancy giggled and pulled her jacket tightly around her. The cold fall air made her shiver even though the sun

1

was shining. Nancy loved being outside with George and Bess. They were her two best friends. Nancy's puppy, Chocolate Chip, was playing nearby.

Chip ran over to Bess and dropped a stick at her feet. Bess patted the puppy and threw the stick for her to fetch. Then she picked at the leaves that were stuck in her long, blond hair.

"Come on," George said. "We promised Bess's grandmother that we'd rake these before tonight. And we still have to get into our Halloween costumes."

Bess's parents were away for the weekend so Bess's grandmother was staying with Bess. Nancy and George were going to sleep over at Bess's house that night.

"Bess!" Nancy called when she saw that Bess wasn't doing her share. Bess was still playing with Chocolate Chip.

"Can I help?" a voice suddenly asked.

Nancy whirled around in surprise. Molly Angelo was standing on the sidewalk behind her. Molly was eight years old, just like Nancy and her friends. She lived down the street from Bess.

"Hi," Bess said. "You want to help? Great! Here, take my rake."

Nancy shook her head as Bess shoved the rake into Molly's hands. Then Bess walked over to sit down on the front steps.

"Thanks," Molly said. She brushed her curly hair out of her eyes.

"Let's rake the leaves into one big pile," Nancy said.

George and Nancy got busy. They raked a lot of the leaves into the center of the yard.

Molly bent down to pat Chocolate Chip. Before she had a chance, Chip ran straight through the pile of leaves. Leaves flew everywhere.

"Chip, stay out of our pile," Nancy scolded.

Then Chip bounded over to the

3

bushes by the porch. She came back and dropped something at Molly's feet.

"Hey, look what I found!" Molly cried.

"What?" Nancy asked, looking up.

Molly held up a strangely shaped key.

Nancy and her friends rushed over to Molly. Nancy had never seen a key like this before. It was at least four inches long, and it looked heavy. The top of the key was shaped like a heart. The rest of the key was twisted into a zig-zag shape. A dirty green ribbon was looped through it. The ribbon was tied in a bow.

"Wow," George said. "That's the craziest-looking key I've ever seen." She reached out to touch it.

"Finders keepers," Molly said. She clutched the key tightly to her chest.

"No way," Bess said. "That belongs to my mom or dad. It was in our yard. And anyway it looks old. It's probably been out here a long time. Give it back."

Molly clutched the key even tighter. "Nancy's dog gave it to me," she said. "So it's mine."

Nancy and George shook their heads.

"No, it's Bess's," Nancy said. "Give it back to her."

Molly pouted, but she handed the key over to Bess. "No fair," she said. Then she turned and stomped away.

"She has a lot of nerve," George said when Molly was gone.

"Well, at least she gave it back. I wonder what this key opens," Bess said. She looked at it closely. "Let's see if my grandmother knows."

Bess hurried toward the house. Nancy and George quickly followed.

"Grammy?" Bess called as she ran into the living room.

"In here," Bess's grandmother answered from the kitchen.

6

Bess raced to the kitchen with the big key in her hand.

Grandma Marvin was in the kitchen, making lollipops. She was going to give them out that night for Halloween.

"Look what we found in the yard," Bess said.

Grandma Marvin's face lit up. "Oh!" she cried. "Look at that!" But then she frowned.

"What's wrong?" Bess asked.

"Oh, nothing," Grandma Marvin said. But she was still frowning.

"Have you ever seen this key before?" Bess asked. "What do you think it opens?"

"Oh, don't ask me," Grandma Marvin said. "I have no idea."

She took the key from Bess and turned it over in her hands. She smoothed out the green ribbon. "It *is* very unusual," she said. "Let's put it in the foyer on the table across from the front door. That way your parents will see it first thing when they come home."

"But it's like a mystery, Grammy," Bess moaned. "We want to know what it opens. And we want to know now."

"Don't be so impatient," Grandma Marvin said. "Isn't it time for Nancy and George to go home? They have to change into their Halloween costumes. It will be time to go out trick-or-treating soon."

Bess nodded. "And you have to get your things for our sleepover tonight," she said to Nancy and George.

"Yay!" Nancy said with excitement.

This was going to be a fun night. First, trick-or-treating. Then a sleepover with Bess and George!

Bess walked Nancy and George to the front door. She put the strange key on a small table in the foyer.

"Hurry back," Bess called as Nancy and George walked down the front steps.

\*       \*       \*

8

Two hours later the girls were all dressed up in their Halloween costumes. Nancy was a witch—but a pretty witch. She let her long reddish blond hair flow out from under her pointy witch's hat, and she didn't wear the ugly green nose that came with her costume.

Bess was dressed up as a movie star. She wore a pink satin gown. She had a long pink feather boa around her neck.

George was a fortune teller. She had wrapped a turban around her dark curly hair, and she carried a crystal ball.

Nancy's father, Carson Drew, walked with the girls as they went trick-or-treating. They started at Bess's next-door neighbor's house.

Nancy, Bess, and George took turns ringing the doorbell. They giggled as they shouted, "Trick or treat!" Then they watched as their bags were filled with candy.

When the girls reached Nancy's street, they ran into Rebecca Ramirez, another third-grader who lived near Nancy. Rebecca wanted to be an actress when she grew up. She was dressed like a movie star, too.

"Watch out," Nancy warned her friends. "Rebecca told me she's going to play a trick on someone tonight."

"A trick?" George asked. "I hope it isn't throwing eggs or squirting shaving cream."

"Nope. She has a bag of flour—don't you?" Nancy said to Rebecca.

"Yes," Rebecca admitted, holding up a small brown bag. "I'm going to toss it at old Mr. Randolph."

"Why would you do that?" Bess asked.

"It's an old-fashioned Halloween prank," Rebecca said. "I saw it in a movie. You throw the flour in a mean person's face."

"Mr. Randolph's not mean," Nancy said.

"Well, last week my ball got lost in his bushes, and he yelled when he saw me looking for it in his yard," Rebecca said. "Now I'm going to get back at him. See you guys later."

"Gee," George whispered to Nancy as Rebecca walked down the street. "I wouldn't want to make Rebecca mad."

Nancy giggled when Rebecca was out of sight. "I would never throw flour in someone's face," she said. "But don't you wish you could be there to see her do it?"

"No," Bess said. "She might get flour on me."

A while later Carson Drew walked the girls back to Bess's house. He waved goodbye as Nancy and her friends started up the driveway.

"This was the best Halloween ever," Bess said. "My candy bag is so full, I can hardly lift it."

11

"Mine, too," George said.

"Come on," Bess said. "Let's go inside and see how much stuff we got."

Bess, George, and Nancy started to walk faster.

Just as they were about to enter the house, Nancy heard a rustling noise in the bushes. An instant later something leaped out at her with a terrible cry!

# 2

## Ghost on the Loose

**N**ancy screamed. She dropped her bag of candy. A ghost was standing right in front of her.

The ghost lifted his arms high in the air. He leaped at Bess.

"Bugga-bugga-booo!" he yelled.

Bess screamed. George screamed, too. But then all three girls saw that the ghost was just a boy in a Halloween costume. They started to laugh.

"Brett, you creep," Bess said. "You scared us!"

"Helloooo," the ghost said.

Nancy stared at the ghost carefully.

A white sheet covered his whole body. There were two holes cut in it for eyes. How did Bess know that it was Brett?

"Who's under there?" Nancy asked, reaching for the sheet.

"It's Brett Sanderson," Bess said. "He told me at school today that he was going to be a ghost."

"Can I come in and have a drink of water?" the ghost asked. "I'm dying of thirst."

"You're already dead," George joked.

"Huh?" the boy said.

"Because you're a ghost," George said with a laugh.

"You can come inside, Brett," Bess said. "My grandmother will get you a glass of water."

The ghost followed the three girls into the house. Bess asked her grandmother if Brett could have a drink.

"Of course," Grandma Marvin told the ghost. "Wait right here."

She hurried to the kitchen to get some water.

Nancy and her friends were shivering.

"Let's go into the den," Bess said. "Grammy built a fire in the fireplace."

The three friends said good-bye to Brett and hurried into the den. They spilled their bags of candy out on the floor.

"I'm not going to count mine," George said. "I'm just going to count what I eat." She opened a small candy bar and popped the whole thing into her mouth. "One."

Nancy giggled. "I'm going to sort mine into four piles," she said. "All the candy bars in one pile. All the gummy candy in another pile. And all the hard candies in the third pile."

"What's the fourth pile for?" Bess asked.

"It's for weird things," Nancy said. "Like that old bruised apple and this small squashed loaf of pumpkin bread. I'm not going to eat that stuff until my dad looks at it."

George looked over at the fourth pile and made a face. "I wouldn't eat it even then!"

The next morning Nancy woke up early. Something was tickling her face.

With her eyes still closed, she reached up and rubbed her cheek. Something fuzzy was crawling on her!

"Help!" Nancy cried. She let out a little scream.

"What?" Bess asked, sitting up in bed.

"What's wrong?" George asked. She was lying on the floor in a sleeping bag beside Nancy.

17

Nancy sat up fast. Then she saw what was tickling her.

It was the long pink feather boa—the one Bess had worn with her Halloween costume the night before. It had fallen off Bess's dresser.

"Your costume is attacking me," Nancy said with a laugh. She pushed the feathery thing away.

"Sorry," Bess said. She hopped out of bed and picked up the feather boa. "I'd better put it away before anything happens to it. Let's go up to the attic and put it back."

"Now? Before breakfast?" George asked, rubbing her eyes.

"Come on, George," Nancy said. She jumped up to follow Bess. "We can eat in a little while. I love attics."

Nancy grabbed her bathrobe and put it on. George climbed out of her sleeping bag and slipped on a pair of warm, woolly slippers. Then they all hurried down the hall to the attic stairs.

Nancy shivered on the way up. The attic was cold. But she didn't care. She liked to explore.

Bess hung the feather boa on a rack of old clothes.

Nancy started to look around.

"Oh, look at this old baby carriage," Nancy said. "It's so cute."

"It was my mom's when she was a baby," Bess said.

George picked up an old wooden tennis racquet. "Tennis, anyone?" she said, swinging it through the air.

"No, thanks," Bess answered. "Let's go back down. I smell pancakes."

Nancy turned toward the stairs. Then she stopped in her tracks. "Hey," she said, pointing, "look at that!"

"What?" Bess asked, following Nancy's gaze.

"That old trunk," Nancy said. "See the shape of the lock? It's a heart, just like the heart shape on the key Chip found."

Bess gasped with excitement. She and George ran over to the trunk.

"You're right!" George said. "And the keyhole is the same size as that crazy old key."

"Wow," Bess said. "My mom is going to be so happy."

"How come?" Nancy asked.

"This trunk has been up here forever," Bess said. "But we never knew where the key was. I bet there's lots of cool stuff in there."

Bess ran down the attic stairs and out into the hallway.

"Grammy? Grammy, guess what," she called from the second floor. "We know what that key is for. Can you bring it up here? I think it will open that trunk in the attic."

There was no answer.

"I guess she can't hear me," Bess said, climbing the stairs again. "Let's just go get it ourselves."

The girls left the attic and hurried down to the foyer.

When they reached the table by the front door, they froze.

"I don't believe it," Bess cried out. "The key is gone!"

# 3

# The Key to the Mystery

It was there yesterday," George said. "It was on the table when we left to go trick-or-treating. I saw it."

"Me, too," Bess said.

"Maybe your grandmother moved it," Nancy said. "Let's go ask her."

"Good idea," Bess said as she headed toward the kitchen.

Grandma Marvin was at the kitchen counter, pouring sugar into a mixing bowl. She was making cookies.

"Sit down, girls," she said as they came in. "Your breakfast is getting cold."

Bess didn't sit down. "Grammy," she said. "Did you take that key? The one we found yesterday? I think it will open the trunk in the attic."

"Hmm?" Grandma Marvin said, still stirring her batter. "Heavens, no. I didn't take the key."

"Then I'm going to look for it again," Bess said, marching out of the kitchen.

George pulled on Nancy's sleeve. "Maybe someone stole it," she said. "Maybe it's a mystery! What do you think?"

"I don't know," Nancy said. She thought for a moment. Who would have wanted the key? Who could have taken it?

"Brett," Nancy mumbled out loud.

"Huh?" George asked.

"I was just thinking," Nancy answered. "We left Brett standing in the foyer last night. Maybe he took the key. I'm going to get my detective's notebook."

Nancy ran up to Bess's bedroom. Her backpack was on the floor near her sleeping bag. She bent down and pulled out her small blue notebook.

Then she hurried back to the kitchen. George and Bess were already at the table, eating pancakes with maple syrup.

"Did you find the key?" Nancy asked Bess as she sat down next to her. She took a bite of her breakfast.

Bess shook her head. "I looked all over the foyer. It's gone."

"That stinks," George said. "How are we going to get into that trunk?"

Nancy ate a few more bites of her pancakes. "We have to find that key."

She opened her notebook to a clean page. At the top she wrote: "The Case of the Missing Key." Then she wrote: "Suspects." Under that, she wrote Brett Sanderson's name.

"Brett is our first suspect," Nancy said.

"You're right," Bess said. "We left him alone by the front door. And so did you, Grammy—when you went to get him a glass of water."

"Why would that boy steal an old, dirty key?" Grandma Marvin asked.

"I know why," George said quickly. "He collects keys."

"He does?" Bess asked. Her eyes opened wide. "How do you know?"

"I've seen them," George announced. "He wears a key ring on his belt almost every day. Whenever he finds an old key, he puts it on his key ring."

Nancy nodded. "Maybe Brett wanted the key because it's so different."

"But who else?" Bess asked. "Do we have any other suspects?"

"Finders keepers," George said.

"What are you talking about?" Bess asked through a mouthful of pancake.

Nancy gave George a smile. "George means Molly Angelo. Remember? She said 'finders keepers' yesterday when she found the key. She was really angry that we made her give it back."

"Oh. Right," Bess agreed.

Nancy wrote Molly's name underneath Brett's in her notebook.

"I don't know, though," Nancy said. "How could Molly have taken the key? She didn't even come into the house."

"Not in the afternoon, she didn't," Bess said. "But what about at night? While we were out trick-or-treating?"

"Could be," Nancy said.

Nancy turned to Grandma Marvin. "Mrs. Marvin, did Molly Angelo come in the house last night during trick-or-treat?"

"I couldn't say for sure," Grandma Marvin answered. "I don't know Molly Angelo. What does she look like?"

"She has long curly dark hair," George answered.

Grandma Marvin shrugged. "I don't know," she said.

Nancy thought hard. She tapped her pencil on her cheek.

"Well, how many trick-or-treaters came *inside* the house last night?" Nancy asked.

Grandma Marvin rolled out the cookie dough on the countertop. "Only one or two," she said. "Most of them just stood on the porch and held out their bags for candy."

"Who came inside?" George asked.

"Oh, mercy me, I don't know," Grandma Marvin said. "Who could tell, with all those masks and costumes?"

Right, Nancy thought. And besides, Bess's grandmother doesn't live in this neighborhood. She wouldn't know many of the kids.

"Let's go back to the foyer and search for clues," Nancy said. "Maybe the thief left something there."

Bess ate the last two bites of her pancakes. Then she jumped up from the table. The girls hurried to the front door.

"Look at that!" George cried out as soon as they reached the small table. "A clue."

"Where?" Nancy asked eagerly.

"Under the table," George said, pointing.

Nancy went over to the table and bent down. She found a lollipop on the floor.

"This isn't a clue," Nancy said. "It's one of the lollipops Bess's grandma made for Halloween. It probably fell out of the candy bowl last night."

"Oh," George said.

Nancy stood up and looked at the table. "But this *is* a clue!" she said suddenly.

Bess ran to see. "What?" she asked.

"This." Nancy pointed to a few specks of white powder on top of the table. "I think it's flour."

"Flour?" George asked. "We know who had flour on Halloween. Rebecca!"

"Exactly," Nancy said, smiling. "Maybe it won't take so long to solve this mystery after all."

Nancy looked back at the table.

Then she heard a terrible sound. Grandma Marvin was screaming for help!

# 4

# Pumpkin Bombs

**N**ancy, Bess, and George ran to the kitchen as fast as they could.

Grandma Marvin screamed again and pointed at the floor. "Get that out of here!"

Nancy's puppy was in front of the refrigerator. Chip was playing with something on the floor. Something gray and yucky.

Then Nancy saw her father. He was standing by the side door.

"Daddy!" Nancy said. "What are you doing here?"

"I came to pick you up, silly," Carson

31

Drew said. "And I brought Chip along for the walk."

"And she brought me a dead mouse!" Grandma Marvin said, still pointing. "Please, take it away."

"Is it really dead?" Nancy asked.

"A mouse?" Bess screamed. "I hate mice! Get me out of here!"

Bess backed away and hopped onto a chair.

Nancy's father shook his head. "That's not a dead mouse," he said. "It's just a chewed-up rubber toy."

Carson Drew bent down and lifted the old rubber toy from the kitchen floor. Nancy let out a sigh of relief. At first glance, it did look real.

"See?" Carson said. "Chocolate Chip must have found this outside. I didn't notice it. But it really scared Bess's grandmother when Chip dropped it at her feet."

"Yuck," Bess said with a shiver. "I

32

don't blame her. It's gross—even if it *is* rubber."

"Well, Pudding Pie?" Carson Drew asked his daughter. Pudding Pie was his nickname for Nancy. "You'd better get dressed. It's time to go."

"Can't I stay a little longer, Daddy?" Nancy said. "We're working on a mystery. We have to find a missing key so we can open an old trunk in Bess's attic."

"Well, that's up to Mrs. Marvin," Carson Drew said. "She might have her hands full with all three of you."

"Oh, no. It's fine with me," Bess's grandmother answered. "Just take the dog and the mouse—please."

Nancy's father laughed. "All right," he said. "See you later."

Nancy gave her puppy a hug and thanked Bess's grandmother. Then all three girls ran upstairs to Bess's room to get dressed.

When she had finished dressing, Nancy picked up her blue notebook. She opened it and wrote inside:

Clues:
Flour on the table. Thief might have had flour on hands.

Then she added Rebecca to her suspect list.

Bess peeked over Nancy's shoulder to see what she was writing.

"Do you really think Rebecca would steal something?" Bess asked when she saw Nancy's notes.

Nancy didn't answer right away. "No," she finally said. "Probably not. But a good detective has to follow the clues."

"And the flour points to Rebecca," Bess announced.

"Right," Nancy said. "But we have other suspects, too. Let's go talk to

Brett first. We know for sure he was in the foyer alone last night."

"*And* he collects keys," George reminded them.

With their jackets zipped up tightly, Nancy, Bess, and George walked to Brett's house. He lived a block away.

"Gross!" George cried when they reached his front yard. "What a mess!"

Nancy couldn't believe it. Someone had taken a big carved pumpkin and smashed it on Brett's front lawn. Broken pieces of pumpkin were smeared all over the walk.

"Who would do that?" Nancy asked, shaking her head. She looked around. Suddenly a small carved pumpkin crashed on the ground beside her.

*Splat!*

"Yikes!" Nancy cried. She jumped out of the way just in time. "Where did that come from?"

35

From the trees, she got her answer. She heard two boys' voices laughing hard.

"Gotcha," Brett called as he jumped out of a tree.

"What were you doing up there?" Bess asked. She put her hands on her hips and glared at him.

"Dropping pumpkin bombs," Brett said with a grin.

"You could have hurt us," Nancy said.

"We weren't going to *hit* you," another voice said.

A moment later Jeff Martin jumped down from the tree. He was Brett's best friend.

"That's yucky," Bess said, pointing to the squashed pumpkin on the sidewalk.

"Don't worry," Brett said. "We're going to clean it up later."

"Well, it's still dangerous," George said. "You'd better stop."

Nancy heard a jingling sound. Right away, she knew what it was.

Keys.

Nancy looked at Brett's belt. A big key ring dangled from it. It had a lot of keys on it. But she didn't see *their* key.

"Uh, listen," Nancy said. "We wanted to ask you something. Did you see a cool-looking key on the table when you were in Bess's house last night?"

Brett twisted his mouth into a funny shape.

"What do you mean?" he said. "I wasn't in Bess's house last night."

"Yes, you were," George said. "You came in for a drink of water. Remember? You were in that ghost costume."

"What ghost costume?" Brett asked.

Bess opened her eyes wide. "Brett Sanderson, you told me you were going to be a ghost for Halloween," she said. "And I saw you. That was you last night. I know it was."

38

"No way," Brett said. "I changed my mind. I decided to be a pirate instead. If you don't believe me, I'll show you my costume."

Nancy and George looked at each other. Nancy didn't know what to think.

"Okay," Bess said. "Show us."

Brett went into his house. A minute later he came out wearing a pirate's hat and carrying a sword. He had the other parts of his costume on a hanger.

Nancy looked at Brett's pirate costume.

"What's that?" she asked, pointing to some white stuff on his black hat and pants.

"That's dried shaving cream," Brett said. "Jeff and I had a shaving cream war last night."

"Yeah," Jeff said. "We were covered in the stuff. It was a lot of fun."

Nancy was quiet for a minute. She remembered seeing some kids squirting shaving cream at each other. One of them might have been Brett.

"I guess that proves it wasn't Brett, right?" Bess asked.

Nancy nodded. "But someone came into your house last night dressed as a ghost. If it wasn't Brett, then who was it?"

# 5

## The Candy Clue

You're right," Bess said to Nancy. "Who could it have been?"

Nancy opened her blue notebook as they walked away from Brett and Jeff. She crossed off Brett's name from her suspect list. Then she added: "Ghost. Who was it?"

"Well, we still have two other suspects—Molly and Rebecca," Nancy said. "Let's go visit one of them."

"Molly lives on my block," Bess said. "Let's go there first."

The girls headed for Molly's house. On the way there, Nancy thought about the mystery. She remembered how badly Molly wanted the crazy key. Maybe she wanted it so much that she came back and took it, Nancy thought.

"We're here," Bess said. She pointed at Molly's house. "What now? Do we just come out and ask her if she stole the key?"

"No," Nancy said. "Leave it to me. I have an idea."

Nancy marched up to Molly's front door and rang the bell. Molly answered it. She was still in her pajamas. They were white with red ribbon trim.

"Hi," Nancy said. "Can we come in?"

"Uh, hi," Molly said. "Sure. What's up?"

"We're trying to solve a mystery," Nancy said as the three girls stepped into Molly's house. She gave a quick wink to Bess and George.

"What kind of mystery?" Molly asked.

"We're trying to find out who dressed

up as a ghost last night for Halloween. Did you see any ghosts?" Nancy asked.

"Sure," Molly said. "I saw three or four different ones. But I don't know who they were."

"Bummer," Bess said. "Because someone came to our house dressed as a ghost and—"

Nancy poked Bess in the ribs. She didn't want Bess to mention the key.

"—and jumped out and scared us," Nancy said, finishing Bess's sentence.

"Ohhhh," Molly said, nodding. "And you want to get back at them."

"Sort of," Nancy said.

Molly smiled. "I know what you mean," she said. "Someone hid in the bushes and tried to scare me last year, too. But I never found out who it was."

Nancy didn't know what else to say. She turned to the front door and started to leave. But then she got another idea. She knew a tricky way to find out a clue about Molly.

"Hey," Nancy said, turning back toward Molly. "Did you get a lot of candy last night?"

"Yeah," Molly said. "Almost a whole bag."

"Wow! Can we see it?" Nancy asked.

"Sure," Molly said. She motioned for them to follow her. "My mom made me put it in a big bowl in the kitchen."

Bess gave Nancy a strange look as they walked toward Molly's kitchen. But Nancy couldn't explain. Not now.

"Tell you later," she whispered to Bess.

In the kitchen, Molly placed a huge glass bowl in front of the three girls. Nancy looked through all the Halloween candy carefully. While she did, Molly ate a piece of chocolate.

"You can have this," Molly said, pushing a box toward the girls. "I hate licorice."

"Thanks," George said, taking the box. "I love it."

When Nancy was finished looking through the bowl, she and her friends said good-bye to Molly.

"Well?" Bess said when they were back on the sidewalk. "What was that all about? Why did you want to see her Halloween candy?"

Nancy smiled. "To get a clue, of course. I wanted to find out if she went trick-or-treating at *your* house last night, Bess. Then we'd know if she could have stolen the key."

"But how could you tell?" Bess asked.

"I checked to see if she had any of the homemade lollipops your grandmother made."

"That was so smart!" George said to Nancy. She smiled at her friend proudly.

"Yeah," Bess agreed with an excited nod. "You're a great detective."

"Did she have any of Grandma Marvin's lollipops?" George asked.

"No," Nancy said, shaking her head.

"So that means Molly is innocent," Bess said.

"Not really," Nancy said. "She still could have done it."

# 6

# Grumpy Grandma

**H**ow could Molly have done it?"
Bess asked. "If she didn't have any
lollipops, then she wasn't at my
house, right?"

"That's what I thought at first,"
Nancy said. "But then I saw Molly
eating some of her candy. That's when
I realized the lollipops weren't a good
clue."

"Why not?" George asked. She
opened up the box of licorice and
popped a piece into her mouth.

"Because she could have gotten a lollipop at Bess's house last night and she

48

could have already eaten it," Nancy said.

"My stomach is growling," Bess said. "Let's not talk about candy. Let's go home and have lunch."

"Yeah," George agreed. "Let's take a break. I'm hungry, too."

Nancy didn't want to investigate the mystery any more just then either. She wanted time to think about the clues. She took out her notebook and looked at the list of suspects again.

Brett's name was crossed off. And Nancy wasn't sure about Molly. There were still two other suspects—Rebecca and the ghost.

I hope Rebecca didn't steal the key, Nancy thought. Rebecca was one of Nancy's friends. The two girls often walked to school together.

Nancy closed her notebook with a sigh.

"What's wrong?" George asked.

"Oh, nothing," Nancy said. "I just wonder if we're ever going to find out what's in that trunk."

"We will," George said. "You're great at solving mysteries." She patted Nancy's arm. "Let's forget about that old key for a while. Come on. I'll race you to the corner. Ready . . . set . . . go!"

With that, George took off running. Nancy did, too. But Bess didn't run. Bess never liked to run if she didn't have to.

In a few seconds, the race was over. George had won. George was a super athlete.

"Hey! Wait for me!" Bess called.

She half ran, half walked the length of the block to catch up with her friends.

"Running really works up an appetite!" she said. "Come on. Let's go in and eat."

Nancy and George laughed and followed Bess into the house. Bess's grandmother had lunch waiting.

"There's chicken noodle soup and grilled cheese sandwiches," Grandma Marvin said.

"Yummy," Bess said as she tossed her jacket on a chair.

"I love grilled cheese," George said.

The girls washed their hands. Then they sat down at the table to eat their lunch.

When their sandwiches were almost finished, the doorbell rang. Bess got up to answer it.

"It's the paper boy," she called from the front door. She came back into the kitchen. "We owe him five dollars," she said as she picked up her grandmother's purse from the counter.

"Oooh, hold it!" Grandma Marvin cried. She jumped up from her chair and grabbed the purse from Bess.

"Don't you know it's not nice to go into other people's things? I'll take care of the paper boy."

Bess's face turned red. "Sorry, Grammy," she said. "Mom always lets me pay him. I thought it would be okay."

Nancy blushed, too. She felt bad that Bess had been scolded in front of her and George.

Grandma Marvin headed toward the front door with her purse.

Nancy stood up. She leaned over and whispered to Bess. "Let's go back outside. Maybe your grandma is tired of having us in the house."

"Good idea," Bess agreed.

"We're going out again," Bess called to her grandmother.

"Fine," Grandma Marvin called back. She had just finished paying the paper boy.

The girls put on their jackets and

headed out the side door. Bess started to skip down the driveway.

The wind blew some dried leaves across the sidewalk. The branches of the bushes and trees rustled.

Then someone leaped out of the bushes and pounced on Bess!

# 7

# The Ghost Returns

Bess screamed.

"Ha, ha," said the boy standing in front of them. "Scared you again!"

Nancy looked at the boy. She didn't know who he was, but she could tell from the look on Bess's face that Bess knew him.

"Ooooh, you creep!" Bess yelled. "How could you do that?"

"Easy," the boy said. "Just like I did last night. I hid in the bushes and waited for you."

"Huh?" George said. "Last night? You were the ghost?"

"Yup," the boy said with a big grin.

"Who is he?" Nancy asked, giving Bess a questioning glance.

"This is Carl," Bess said. "He's a sixth-grader. He's our paper boy."

Oh, Nancy thought. No wonder Bess knew him. He must have hid in the bushes while we were putting on our jackets.

Nancy eyed Carl up and down. He was short for a sixth-grader.

Now we'll find out what really happened last night, Nancy thought.

"Why did you pretend to be Brett?" Nancy asked him.

"I didn't," Carl said, still grinning. "You called me Brett. I never *said* I was Brett."

"Nancy," George whispered. "Ask him about the key."

Nancy nodded and cleared her throat. "When you came in the house last night, there was a special key on the table. Did you take it?" Nancy asked.

"No way," Carl answered. "I saw it, but I didn't take it."

Nancy squinted at him. He had a funny look on his face. She thought he was hiding something.

"Then why did you ask to come in the house?" Nancy asked.

Carl's grin grew even bigger. "It's a trick I have," he admitted. He looked really pleased with himself. "I do it every year on Halloween."

"What trick?" Bess demanded.

"I go to lots of houses and ask for a drink of water," Carl explained. "People are friendly on Halloween. They always say yes. They leave me standing by the front door alone. And guess what? They leave the candy bowl, too! So while they're gone, I help myself to big handfuls of candy. It works every time."

"That's not nice," George said.

Carl laughed. "You should see how much candy I got," he bragged. "I could hardly carry it home."

"But what about the key?" Nancy asked. "Are you sure you didn't take it?"

"Why would I want an old key?" Carl replied.

Nancy didn't have an answer for that. And besides, she was sure he was telling the truth. Why would he lie about the key? He had already admitted being a major candy thief!

"Okay," Nancy said.

"Just watch out, Bess," Carl said. He laughed again. You never know who's going to get you!"

Bess turned away from Carl. Nancy could tell that she really didn't like him.

When Carl was gone, Nancy started down the driveway again. "Come on," she said to Bess and George. "I guess we only have one suspect left—Rebecca. Let's go to her house and see what we can find out."

"Okay," Bess said.

After the girls had walked two blocks, Nancy felt a drop of rain on her cheek. She looked up at the gray sky.

"Do you feel rain?" Nancy asked.

"Yes," George said. "It looks like it's going to pour."

"I don't want to get rained on," Bess said. "Let's go back to my house."

Nancy shrugged. "Okay. Maybe we can call Rebecca instead."

When the girls arrived back at Bess's house, Nancy went straight to the phone and dialed Rebecca's number. Rebecca's mother answered.

"Hello," Nancy said. "This is Nancy. May I please speak to Rebecca?"

"Oh, hi, Nancy," Mrs. Ramirez said. "Rebecca is sick with the flu. She's resting in bed."

"She's sick?" Nancy said, surprised. Rebecca had seemed fine the night before.

"Hold on a second," Mrs. Ramirez said. "I think she's awake. I'll take the phone to her room so she can talk to you."

A moment later Rebecca said hello. She quickly explained to Nancy what had happened.

"I was just starting to go trick-or-treating when I saw you last night," Rebecca said in a scratchy voice. "A minute later I felt really sick. My mom took me straight home. I didn't even get any candy."

"That's awful," Nancy said. She felt bad for Rebecca. "I guess you didn't get to do your flour prank, either?"

"No," Rebecca said, sounding unhappy.

"Well, maybe you can do it next year," Nancy said. "Get better soon."

She hung up and explained everything to Bess and George.

"Now what?" George asked.

Nancy shook her head. She didn't have any ideas left.

Grandma Marvin appeared in the

doorway with a tray in her hands. "Such serious faces," she said. "How about some fresh cookies to cheer you up?"

Grandma Marvin put the tray of cookies on a table in the living room. There were three small glasses of milk, too. Then she left the room.

"Yum," Bess said. Her face lit up. "Cut-out cookies!"

"I love these," George said, reaching for a heart-shaped cookie.

Nancy picked up a cookie, too. Hers was shaped like a horse. It had sprinkles on the mane and tail.

After Nancy took a bite she noticed her fingertips were white. She turned the cookie over. There was flour on the bottom.

"Hey!" she cried out. "I think I know who took the key!"

# 8

# The Cookie Clue

**Y**ou know who took the key?" Bess asked Nancy. Her cookie was halfway to her mouth.

Nancy nodded. A small smile crept across her face.

"I think it was your grandmother." She leaned in closer to Bess and George. She didn't want Grandma Marvin to hear.

"But why?" Bess asked.

"I don't know why," Nancy said softly. "But this—" Nancy held up her cookie. "This is the proof."

Bess and George looked puzzled.

63

"See the flour?" Nancy whispered. She turned her cookie over and showed them the flour on the bottom. "Your grandma was making cookies this morning when we found the trunk in the attic."

"So?" Bess said.

"Don't you remember?" Nancy went on. "She didn't answer us when we asked her to bring up the key. So we came down to get it ourselves. By then it was gone. I think your grandma took the key. When she picked it up she dropped flour on the table."

Nancy could see Bess thinking about what had happened. "But I still don't know why she would take the key. She knew we wanted it."

"Me, either," Nancy said.

"Let's ask her," George said.

"Good idea," Bess said, standing up. "But we can't ask her if she *stole* it."

"I'll just ask her if she *took* it," Nancy said.

Nancy stood up straight and marched into the kitchen. The other girls followed her. Grandma Marvin was washing the mixing bowls.

"Um, Mrs. Marvin," Nancy said politely, "I know we asked you once before, but did you take that old key from the table by the front door?"

Grandma Marvin wrinkled her nose. "What would make you think that?" she asked slowly.

"Well, we've been following the clues," Nancy said. "For one thing, I don't think the key was missing last night. Carl, the paper boy, saw it on the table when he came in the house for a drink of water. And he was one of the last trick-or-treaters."

"Yes," Grandma Marvin said. "Go on."

"Also, I found flour on the table it was on," Nancy said. "I remembered that you were baking cookies this morning. You must have had flour on your hands when you took the key."

Grandma Marvin was quiet for a long time. She stared at Nancy with her head tilted to the side. Finally she nodded and gave Nancy a tiny smile.

"You're right, Nancy," Grandma Marvin said. "I did take the key. It's in my purse. That's why I didn't want you to pay the paper boy, Bess. I didn't want you to see the key."

"Why, Grammy?" Bess cried.

Grandma Marvin wiped her hands on a dish towel and sighed. "Well, you see, girls, that trunk in the attic belongs to me. When you found the key, I didn't want you to open it," she said, "because there's something very special in there for you, Bess. I've been saving it for years to give to you. It was going to be a surprise."

"Ohhh," Nancy and Bess both said at the same time. George just stared at her feet.

"Gee, I'm sorry we ruined your surprise," Nancy said to Grandma Marvin.

"Well, I guess this is as good a time as any," Grandma Marvin said.

She walked over to her purse and opened it. She took out the crazy-looking old key.

"Come on. Let's go up to the attic."

"Really?" Bess cried, clapping her hands.

Quickly, the girls followed Mrs. Marvin to the attic stairs. Then one by one they climbed up.

At the top, Bess's grandmother kneeled down beside the trunk. She turned to Nancy.

"There are so many treasures in here," she said. "And we haven't been able to get it open for a long time. Thank you for finding the key."

"Oh, I didn't find it," Nancy said. "My dog, Chip, did."

Grandma Marvin's eyes opened wide.

"The one with the mouse? Well, I guess I'll have to forgive her, then."

Nancy laughed and stepped back to watch. So did George. Bess leaned in closer to see her surprise.

A moment later Grandma Marvin opened the trunk. There was a beautiful china doll right on top. She lifted it out and handed it to Bess.

"Here you go," she said warmly, giving the doll to Bess. "I think you're old enough to take care of her now. She was mine when I was a girl."

"I love it!" Bess said. She held the doll carefully.

Nancy looked at the doll. Her hair was blond like Bess's. She wore a pink organza dress with white ribbons. She had white satin slippers on her feet.

"Oh, thank you, Grammy. Thank you!" Bess cried, giving her grandmother a big hug.

The girls explored in the trunk a bit longer. They found another dress for

the doll and a tea set. The cups and plates were decorated with tiny pink roses. Soon it was time for Nancy and George to go.

When Nancy got home, she found Chocolate Chip eagerly waiting for her. The puppy jumped up on Nancy and wagged her tail.

"Hi, Chip," Nancy said. She bent down and let the puppy lick her face. "I missed you, too. It feels as though I've been gone a long time, even though it was only overnight."

Nancy gave Chocolate Chip a treat. "Good puppy," she said. "That's your reward for finding the missing key."

Then Nancy went upstairs to her room. She took out her blue notebook and opened it to the Case of the Missing Key. At the bottom she wrote:

Today I solved the Case of the Missing Key. We found out what was inside the trunk. We also spoiled a surprise. It was fun to solve the mystery. But I found out that some mysteries are not supposed to be solved. Not right away, anyway. From now on I'll be a little more careful when I go snooping around!

Case closed.

# TAKE A RIDE
# WITH THE KIDS ON BUS FIVE!

Natalie Adams and James Penny have just started
third grade. They like their teacher, and they like
Maple Street School. The only trouble is, they have
to ride bad old Bus Five to get there!

### #1 THE BAD NEWS BULLY
Can Natalie and James stop the bully on Bus Five?

### #2 WILD MAN AT THE WHEEL
When Mr. Balter calls in sick,
the kids get some strange new drivers.

### #3 FINDERS KEEPERS
The kids on Bus Five keep losing things.
Is there a thief on board?

### #4 I SURVIVED ON BUS FIVE
Bad luck turns into big fun
when Bus Five breaks down in a rainstorm.

# BY MARCIA LEONARD
## ILLUSTRATED BY JULIE DURRELL

A MINSTREL® BOOK
Published by Pocket Books

1237-02

# FULL HOUSE™

# Michelle

**#1: THE GREAT PET PROJECT** 51905-0/$3.50

**#2: THE SUPER-DUPER SLEEPOVER PARTY**
51906-9/$3.50

**#3: MY TWO BEST FRIENDS** 52271-X/$3.50

**#4: LUCKY, LUCKY DAY** 52272-8/$3.50

**#5: THE GHOST IN MY CLOSET** 53573-0/$3.50

**#6: BALLET SURPRISE** 53574-9/$3.50

**#7: MAJOR LEAGUE TROUBLE** 53575-7/$3.50

**#8: MY FOURTH-GRADE MESS** 53576-5/$3.50

**#9: BUNK 3, TEDDY, AND ME** 56834-5/$3.50

**#10: MY BEST FRIEND IS A MOVIE STAR!**
(Super Edition) 56835-3/$3.50

**#11: THE BIG TURKEY ESCAPE** 56836-1/$3.50

A MINSTREL® BOOK

Published by Pocket Books